A Salmon for Simon

W9-AVX-141

Text copyright © 1978 by Betty Waterton
Illustrations copyright © 1978 by Ann Blades
First Meadow Mouse Paperback edition 1990
First revised Meadow Mouse Paperback edition 1996
Seventeenth printing 2011

All rights reserved. No part of this publication may be reproduced, stored in a
retrieval system or transmitted, in any form or by any means, without the prior
written consent of the publisher or a licence from The Canadian Copyright
Licensing Agency (Access Copyright). For an Access Copyright licence,
visit www.accesscopyright.ca or call toll free to 1-800-893-5777.

Groundwood Books / House of Anansi Press
110 Spadina Avenue, Suite 801, Toronto, Ontario M5V 2K4
or c/o Publishers Group West
1700 Fourth Street, Berkeley, CA 94710

We acknowledge for their financial support of our publishing program the Canada
Council for the Arts, the Government of Canada through the Canada Book Fund
(CBF) and the Ontario Arts Council.

 Canada Council   Conseil des Arts
for the Arts   du Canada

 ONTARIO ARTS COUNCIL
CONSEIL DES ARTS DE L'ONTARIO

Library and Archives Canada Cataloguing in Publication
Waterton, Betty
A salmon for Simon
Rev. ed.
"A Meadow Mouse paperback".
ISBN: 978-0-88899-276-5
I. Blades, Ann. II. Title.
PS8595.A796S3 1996   jC813'.54   C96-930824-8
PZ7.W37Sa 1996

Printed and bound in China

A Salmon for Simon

STORY BY
BETTY WATERTON

PICTURES BY
ANN BLADES

A Meadow Mouse Paperback

Groundwood Books * House of Anansi Press

Toronto Berkeley

All summer Simon had been fishing for a salmon.

"It's the king of the fishes," he told his sisters.

"We know," they said. "That's why great-grand-mother calls it Sukai."

When Simon was little, his sisters had taught him how to catch minnows with a strainer. But this year his father had given him a fishing pole of his own, and he had been fishing every day.

He hadn't caught a single salmon.

Now it was September. It was the time of year when many salmon were swimming past the island where Simon lived, near the West Coast of Canada. They were returning from the sea, looking for the rivers and streams where they had been born. There they would lay their eggs so that more salmon could be born.

One day, when the tide was on its way out, Simon and his sisters went clam-digging. When their pail was full, his sisters took the clams home to their mother to cook for supper, but Simon stayed on the beach. He had his fishing pole with him, as he had every day that summer.

"I'm going to stay and fish for a salmon," he said.

And he did.

He sat on a rock and fished.

He sat on a dock and fished.

But he didn't even see a salmon.

He saw red and purple starfish sticking to the rocks.

He saw small green crabs scuttling among the seaweed.

He saw flat white sand dollars lying on the wet sand.

He saw pink sea anemones waving, pale jellyfish floating, and shiners swimming.

But he didn't see a salmon.

"Are they ever hard to catch," thought Simon. He decided to stop fishing, maybe forever.

Simon walked back along the beach to the place where he and his sisters had been clam-digging. The sea water had oozed up from the bottom of the hole and filled it. Some seagulls sat beside it. When Simon came near, they flew up into the air, crying, *"Keer, keer, keer."*

"I'm not good at catching salmon, but I am a good clam-digger," thought Simon.

He dug a few clams and put them on a nearby rock. The gulls flew down, picked up the clams in their beaks, carried them into the air and then dropped them. The clams hit the rocks, and the shells broke open.

Simon listened to the *bang, bang, pop* as they shattered. He watched the gulls fly down and eat the soft clam meat.

Then Simon heard something different, something that sounded like *flap, flap, flap*.

"What's that?" he cried, but nobody answered.

He heard it again—*flap, flap, flap*—and this time the sound was right above his head.

"Keer, keer," shrieked the seagulls, flying off. Simon looked up, and there, not very high above him, was an eagle. Its strong black wings beat the air as it climbed toward the treetops.

Simon had often seen bald eagles, but this one was different, for it was carrying something in its talons—something that glistened.

"A fish!" cried Simon. "He's got a fish!"

He was so excited that he began hopping about and flapping his arms like eagle wings. The seagulls were excited, too, and they circled overhead, screeching.

In all the stir and confusion, the eagle dropped the fish. Down it came out of the sky...

down...

down...

down...

SPLAAT...SPLASH

into the clam hole!

The fish lay on its side in the shallow water and did not move.

Simon ran over. "It's dead," he cried.

But just then the fish flicked its tail and flipped over. Its gills opened and closed, and its fins began to move slowly.

"It's alive," shouted Simon. Then he looked closer. His eyes grew round. "It's alive and it's a *salmon*. This must be the most beautiful fish in the whole world," he thought.

For it was a coho, or silver salmon, that had come from far out in the Pacific Ocean to find the stream where it had been born. It had grown big in the ocean, and strong.

All summer Simon had been waiting to catch just such a fish, and here was one right in front of him. Yet he didn't feel happy.

He watched the big handsome fish pushing its nose against the gravelly sides of the clam hole, trying to find a way out, and he felt sorry for it. He knew it would die if it didn't have enough water to swim in.

Simon wanted the salmon to be safe in the sea where it could swim and leap and dive. He didn't know how he was going to save the salmon, but he had to find a way.

"I won't let you die, Sukai," said Simon.

Simon thought of carrying the fish to the sea, but he knew it was too big and heavy and too slippery for him to pick up.

He thought about waiting for the tide to come in, but he knew the salmon couldn't wait that long.

He looked up at the circling seagulls, but all they said was *"Keer, keer."*

Then, as he looked around, Simon noticed his clam shovel. An idea popped into his head.

He would dig a channel for the salmon to swim down to the sea. That was what he had to do.

Simon began to dig. The wet sand was heavy.

He dug and dug.

After a while he stopped and looked to see how far he had gone, but he had not gone very far at all. He kept on digging.

His mother called him for supper, but he couldn't go because he hadn't finished yet.

The salmon was lying quietly now in the shallow water, waiting.

The sun dipped low in the sky, and the air became cool. Simon's hands were red and he was getting a blister, but he kept on digging.

At last, just when he thought he couldn't lift another shovelful of sand, he looked up and there he was, at the sea.

The channel was finished.

Cold sea water flowed into the pool. When the salmon felt the freshness of the sea, it began to move again. Its nose found the opening to Simon's channel and slowly, slowly the salmon began to swim down it.

Down, down the channel it swam.

At last it reached the open sea.

The salmon dived deep into the cool water, and then, gleaming in the last rays of the setting sun, it suddenly gave a great leap into the air.

And it seemed to Simon that the salmon flicked its tail, as if to say thank you, before it disappeared beneath the waves.

"Goodbye, Sukai," called Simon.

The salmon was free at last.

Soon it would be in the deep, secret places of the sea.

Now the sun had set and a chilly wind was starting to blow. Simon's hands were sore, and his feet were cold, but he felt warm inside. He picked up his fishing pole and his shovel and started for home.

He knew that his house would be bright and cheery inside, because lamplight shone golden through the windows.

And he knew that it would be nice and warm, because he could see smoke curling out of the chimney.

And he knew that something good was cooking for supper, because he could smell a delicious smell.

And Simon thought, as he opened the door, that maybe he would go fishing again tomorrow, after all.

But not for a salmon.